MW01071149

Rebekah – Girl Detective

Books 13 - 16

PJ Ryan

Copyright © 2014 PJ Ryan

Cover Illustration by Carolina Storni

All rights reserved.

ISBN: 0615996647

ISBN-13: 978-0615996646

Contents

"Rebekah - Girl Detective" is a short story series for children ages 9-12 with the remaining titles to be published on a regular basis. Each title can be read on its own.

You can join Rebekah's fun Facebook page for young detectives here:

http://www.facebook.com/RebekahGirlDetective

I'd really love to hear from you!

I very much appreciate your reviews and comments so thank you in advance for taking a moment to leave one for "Rebekah - Girl Detective: Books 13-16."

Sincerely,
PJ Ryan

All bundled sets are also available in paperback from Amazon. Check the author page here for the complete listing:

http://pjryanbooks.com/

Current series:

Rebekah – Girl Detective

RJ – Boy Detective

Mouse's Secret Club

Rebekah, Mouse & RJ: Special Editions

Additionally several PJ Ryan titles are now available as audiobooks and you can also find those listed at the page above.

Rebekah - Girl Detective #13

The
Ghost Snowman

PJ Ryan

Rebekah - Girl Detective #13
The Ghost Snowman

Chapter 1

Rebekah was very excited as she threw the last few things she needed to pack into her suitcase. It was already filled with extra sweaters, thick socks and a few scarves.

She was getting ready to leave on her annual ski trip with her family. But it wasn't just her parents that were going this year. Her cousin RJ, who was a few years older, was going along on the trip too.

She was so excited to see him, not just because he was her cousin, but because he had taught her everything she knew about being a girl detective!

RJ was a detective too and he solved mysteries in the middle of the great big city where he lived. Rebekah and RJ didn't get to see each other too often during the school year, so this ski trip was a very special treat.

Rebekah couldn't wait to tell him about all of the mysteries she had solved in her little town, where she was known as the best detective around.

When they picked up RJ in the city, he was excited too.

"Hi Rebekah!" he said happily as he climbed into the car beside her. "I see you're ready for the slopes," he laughed as he tugged at the bright pink earmuffs she was wearing.

"We're going to have to stay warm," Rebekah said with a grin. "Here, I got some for you too," she laughed. "They'll match your hat."

RJ always wore a detective hat. He had them in many different colors. As a seasoned kid detective, RJ was always on the look-out for mysteries, just like Rebekah was.

"Do you think that we'll find a mystery at the ski lodge?" Rebekah asked with a grin.

"I don't know," RJ replied with a shrug. "But if we do, I'm sure we'll be able to solve it!"

The drive to get to the ski lodge was pretty long. They had to drive along curved roads that got higher and higher as they drove. Rebekah and RJ didn't even notice the distance, because they were talking the whole time.

RJ told her about Joey, his friend, who he solved mysteries with. Rebekah told him about the mysteries she had solved at school. Then they both talked about Mouse's Secret Club, which they both belonged to.

Mouse, Rebekah's best friend, started the club. It was all about pranks.

By the time they were close to the ski lodge, RJ and Rebekah were laughing loudly in the back seat of the car. Rebekah's mother looked at them through the rear view mirror and grinned.

"We're not even there yet and they're already having a great time," she smiled happily.

"I can't wait to get on the slopes," Rebekah's father said. "We're supposed to get some snow while we're up there too kids," he called back over his shoulder. "So you'll get to build some snowmen."

"We're too old for building snowmen," Rebekah said with a sigh.

"No one is ever too old for building snowmen," Rebekah's mother said and laughed.

Chapter 2

When they arrived at the ski lodge, the sun was shining brightly. It made the snow sparkle. There was nothing that Rebekah liked more than the sight of the sun shining on the snow. There was still plenty of time for them to get out on to the slopes and Rebekah couldn't wait.

"Guys go ahead and get settled in, put your stuff away, then we have you set up to meet with an instructor so you can get skiing right away!" Rebekah's Dad said as he handed them each their suitcases.

"Dad we don't need a ski instructor," Rebekah frowned impatiently. "We already know how to ski."

"It's important to get a good reminder," her father said sternly. "If you want to ski, you have to go to the lesson. Understand?" he looked from Rebekah to RJ and back to Rebekah again.

"Yes Dad," Rebekah said with a sigh. They hurried to put their things away in the three bedroom cabin Rebekah's parents had rented for the weekend. There was plenty of room, and the fireplace in the living room kept the whole cabin toasty.

They bundled up in their coats and ski pants and hurried out to the bunny slope. That was where their instructor was waiting for them.

Rebekah thought he was a little strange because he was wearing a very fuzzy tall snow hat with big ears shaped like dog ears hanging off the side.

"Hi, I'm Matt, I'll be your ski instructor," he said cheerfully as he looked from Rebekah to RJ.

"We don't really need much instruction," Rebekah explained. "We've been skiing before." She wanted to get out on the slopes as soon as possible.

"Well it's always good to brush up on safety rules," Matt said firmly, although he was still smiling brightly. "So let's do our best to pay attention and follow the rules!" When he clapped his hands, the floppy ears on his hat shook back and forth.

Rebekah shot a funny look at RJ. RJ shot a funny look back at Rebekah. Then they both looked back at Matt.

Chapter 3

"Okay so there are three big rules of ski slope safety," Matt said cheerfully, his ears still flapping. "First, the whistles," he said as he held up two bright yellow whistles on necklaces. "It's easy to get lost on the slopes, especially if it's snowing. So you two need to make sure that you wear these at all times," he said firmly and handed them each one of the whistles.

"Thanks," Rebekah said and put on the necklace. RJ tried to put on his but it got stuck on his hat. He tugged harder and it finally went down over the hat.

"Thanks," he said quickly. "Now can we start skiing?"

"Wait a minute there little fellow," Matt said with a laugh and held up his gloved hands in the air.

"Little fellow?" RJ whispered to Rebekah with a frown. Rebekah tried not to laugh.

"There's a few more rules we need to talk about," Matt said as he paced back and forth in front of them.

"Now must of the time that you're on the slopes you're going to be on skis. But, if you happen to be walking on the slopes instead of skiing, please be very careful. The slopes are very slippery. One misstep and you could find yourself rolling all the way down to the bottom!" he shook his head at that.

"That sounds like fun," Rebekah said with a smile.

"No," Matt shook his head again. "Not fun. Dangerous little lady," he said and pointed his finger right at her. Rebekah's eyes widened. When Matt turned around, she looked over at RJ.

"Little lady?!" she rolled her eyes. RJ tried not to laugh.

"Now the last rule is the most important rule," Matt said sternly as he turned back. "These slopes are big. There are lots of trees around here. It's very easy to get lost. That's why you must always have a buddy when you ski. Always," he added as he looked at the two of them. "You should ski together and stay together at all times," he said sternly. "Understand?"

RJ and Rebekah nodded. They were familiar with all of the safety rules already so it wasn't hard for them to remember them again.

"Oh and there's one last thing," Matt said as he turned back to the two who were trying not to laugh over their instructor's comments. "Never, ever," he looked into Rebekah's eyes and then into RJ's eyes. "And I mean, ever, go outside after dark," he said in a very serious tone accompanied by a grim frown.

"What?" RJ asked skeptically. "Why?" he studied Matt.

"Oh you haven't heard?" Matt asked in a serious whisper. He wiggled his eyebrows a little.

"Heard what?" Rebekah asked with a raised eyebrow.

"About the ghost snowman," Matt said, still whispering. "That doesn't surprise me. Most of the staff that work here don't like to talk about it. But I wouldn't want you two to run into him by mistake."

"A ghost snowman?" RJ laughed out loud at that. "That's not possible. It doesn't even make sense."

"Believe what you want," Matt shrugged as he looked at RJ. "But if you're not careful, he might catch you."

"Catch us?" Rebekah shuddered a little. "Why would a ghost snowman want to catch us?"

"Okay, I guess I'll have to tell you the whole story," Matt said with a frown. "You see long ago, before this place was a ski lodge, there was a ghost that lived here. A ghost snowman," he added.

"Because that makes sense," RJ rolled his eyes. Rebekah kicked him with her ski boot.

"Just listen," she whispered to him.

Chapter 4

"The story goes that he was once a lonely old man who got lost in the middle of a blizzard. He turned into a snowman and wandered the slopes. When the ski lodge was built, the ghost snowman got mad. He didn't like all the banging and all of the people that were disturbing his snow," Matt explained.

"So he decided he would start capturing people from the ski lodge. He figured that if enough people went missing the ski lodge would have to close," Matt shrugged as if it made perfect sense to him.

"But it's still open," Rebekah pointed out. She found the story to be interesting, but she didn't really believe it.

"Well after the first few people were found shivering in the cold, everyone was told not to go outside of the cabins or the ski lodge at night.

The snowman ghost can only capture people at night, because he never goes out during the day. You know, snowmen and sunshine don't get along," Matt explained. "So to this day we warn everyone that stays here not to go out at night."

Rebekah tilted her head to the side as she thought about the story. She was pretty certain that a ghost snowman would want to avoid the sun if possible. Still, it was hard to believe.

RJ sighed and looked right at Matt. "Can we ski now?"

"Sure you can," Matt said with a shrug. "Just remember, don't go out at night!" Matt said in an eerie voice.

"We'll remember," Rebekah said, but her eyes were gleaming with excitement. As they got their skis on she whispered to RJ. "Sounds like a mystery to me!"

"Ghosts aren't a mystery," RJ shook his head as he snapped on his skis. "They don't exist."

Chapter 5

RJ and Rebekah decided to race down the ski slopes. Rebekah had a little more experience skiing, but RJ was a little bigger and heavier than Rebekah. So the race was pretty close.

When they reached the bottom of the hill, it didn't matter who won. They went right back up the hill to race again.

They had a lot of fun, but the whole time Rebekah's mind was on the snowman ghost.

Rebekah's mother was waiting with some hot cocoa. One with marshmallows for Rebekah, and one with cinnamon for RJ.

As RJ and Rebekah sipped their hot cocoa and warmed up in front of the fire they chatted about how much fun they had skiing.

"But can you believe that ski instructor?" RJ laughed. "Who ever heard of a ghost snowman?"

"Well, if he told us about it, then I bet other people believe it too," Rebekah grinned with a sparkle in her eyes. "What could it hurt to investigate?"

"Rebekah you're not really thinking there's a ghost snowman, are you?" RJ asked with a disapproving frown.

"Maybe not," Rebekah shrugged. "But it sounds like there might be some people that do believe there's a ghost snowman. So why shouldn't we look into it? We're here!"

"Good point," RJ laughed. "I guess we could check it out. He did say that the ghost snowman only comes out at night, so we'll have to go after dark."

"I say we take a quick nap and then sneak out after it gets dark," Rebekah said with a nod.

"It's going to be cold," RJ reminded her.

"Well that's what we have these lovely ear muffs for," Rebekah giggled.

"Another good point," RJ grinned and took a big gulp of his cocoa.

"Isn't that hot?" Rebekah asked with wide eyes.

"Yes, yes it is," RJ squeaked out. His cheeks were very red. After they finished their cocoa they went to their rooms to see if they could get a little sleep before heading out to investigate the mystery of the ghost snowman.

Chapter 6

When Rebekah lay down on her bed, she had a hard time falling asleep at first. She was excited to investigate with RJ, which was something she didn't get to do all that often.

She also was curious about the ghost snowman. Like RJ she didn't really believe in ghosts, but she was sure there had to be a story behind the ghost story. Maybe it was some kind of rare animal that no one had discovered before.

If she and RJ were able to capture it, they might be on the news! Maybe it was a yeti, a strange creature said to wander very snowy areas. Or maybe it was just another ghost story.

As she sorted through all of these ideas, she finally fell asleep.

While Rebekah slept, she dreamed of being out on the slopes all by herself. She was in the middle of a snowstorm. Everything was white everywhere she looked. Not only was it white, it was very very cold. The wind was blowing loudly and snow was swirling all around her.

"Rebekah!" she heard a voice call out from the swirling snow. "Rebekah!"

"Where are you?" Rebekah shouted back. She tried to see through the snow, but it kept blowing in her eyes. She was so very cold.

She suddenly realized she was wearing a bathing suit and flip flops. No wonder she was so cold! She was still wondering why she had chosen to dress for summer in the middle of winter, when she heard the voice again.

"Rebekah!" the voice called out. Rebekah was sure it was the ghost snowman calling to her. She had to find him! As she ran through the snow, she kept hearing her name called again and again.

"Rebekah!" the ghost snowman sounded annoyed that she hadn't found him yet. "Rebekah!" now he sounded a lot like RJ. Rebekah opened her eyes and looked right up into RJ's face.

"Sheesh, you are a deep sleeper," he said with a shake of his head. "I've been trying to wake you up for five minutes."

"Sorry," Rebekah said sleepily as she checked to make sure she wasn't actually in her swimsuit.

"It's time to go," he said in a whisper. "Your Mom and Dad are asleep and I've got the flashlights."

"Okay," Rebekah nodded and rubbed her eyes for a minute. "We need to make sure we bundle up."

Once they had on few sweaters, thick jackets and ski pants, they were ready to sneak out.

"I'm not sure I'll fit through the door," Rebekah giggled quietly as she was so bundled up that she could barely cross her arms.

"Shh," RJ reminded her. "We don't want to get caught before we even get out the door."

Rebekah nodded.

Chapter 7

Once they were outside, the cold hit them hard. Rebekah wished she had worn a ski mask to keep her face warm. She pulled down her hat and adjusted her ear muffs. RJ fixed his detective's hat and pressed his earmuffs hard against his ears.

"Stay close to me," he said sternly. RJ was only a little older than Rebekah, but he did like to act like he was in charge. Rebekah didn't mind, she was just excited to be solving another mystery with him.

As they walked out across the snow toward the ski slopes, Rebekah was amazed by how clear and bright the sky was. There were a lot of stars to see. She was glad they hadn't missed out on seeing them. RJ and Rebekah shined their flashlights in front of them to make sure that they wouldn't trip on anything.

"Why do you think people think it is a ghost snowman?" Rebekah asked with a frown. "It's kind of an odd thing to think of as a ghost."

"Look," RJ pointed his flashlight toward the trees. "Do you see that?" he asked in a whisper.

Rebekah pointed her flashlight in the same direction. She saw what looked like the outline of a figure. A very round figure.

"It's the ghost!" Rebekah said with surprise. "We found that fast!" she laughed.

"It looks like a ghost," RJ agreed as he walked bravely toward it. "But really it's just a snowman," he said as they reached it. "See?" he pointed to the carrot nose sticking out of the face of the snowman.

"People probably spot these at night and think they are ghosts, when they're really just snowmen left over from people making them during the day," he shook his head with a smile. "Ghost snowman mystery solved!"

"Well that wasn't much of a mystery," Rebekah frowned with disappointment.

"Did you really think there would be a ghost to find?" RJ asked. He put his flashlight under his chin so that his face glowed. "Watch out Rebekah! I'm a ghost! I'm going to get you!" he ooohed like a ghost.

Rebekah rolled her eyes and picked up some snow in her gloved hands. She mashed it into a snowball and threw it at RJ. RJ gasped and was scooping up some snow to throw one back at her, when Rebekah froze.

Chapter 8

"Shh, listen," Rebekah said as she grabbed RJ's arm. RJ stopped and listened closely. "Do you hear that?" Rebekah asked. They both heard crunching.

"It sounds like footsteps," RJ whispered back and glanced over his shoulder. "I can't see anyone."

"Maybe it's the ghost snowman!" Rebekah gasped and grabbed RJ's arm tighter.

"Rebekah," RJ sighed and narrowed his eyes. "Ghosts don't have feet. How could they make the sounds of footsteps?"

"Maybe this one does," Rebekah said with a frown. "What else could it be?"

"I don't know," RJ frowned. "But let's take a look."

He and Rebekah walked toward the sound of the footsteps. The closer they got to the sound, the more nervous Rebekah became. She didn't normally believe in ghosts, but the way Matt had talked about the ghost snowman made her wonder.

Suddenly the crunching stopped. RJ shined his flashlight around the snow covered ground.

"Look," RJ said in a hushed voice as he shined the flashlight on one spot.

"What is it?" Rebekah asked as she looked more closely. "Footprints!" she gasped. There were several of them in the snow. "They must belong to the ghost snowman."

"Rebekah-" RJ began to say.

"RJ hush," Rebekah insisted. "Let's follow the footprints, maybe we'll find the ghost, or whatever made the footprints that's not a ghost," she rolled her eyes. RJ nodded and they began to follow the footprints. They didn't hear the crunching anymore. But suddenly they heard another strange sound. It was a howling sound.

"Oh that sounds ghostly," Rebekah said with a shiver.

"I think you mean ghastly," RJ corrected her.

"No, I mean ghostly," Rebekah said as the howl came again.

"I don't think it's a ghost," RJ said. "But it does sound pretty eerie." Rebekah nodded in agreement. They continued to follow the footsteps for a little ways before they heard the howling again, only louder this time. It was so loud that it made Rebekah jump. She shined her flashlight in the direction of the howling.

"There it is again," she murmured. "That ghost is noisy."

"It can't be a ghost," RJ insisted with a stomp of his foot.

"Well let's go see what it is," Rebekah suggested bravely. "The footprints have stopped anyway," Rebekah pointed out as she shined her flashlight on the ground. "This must be where the ghost stopped walking and started floating."

"Or it could be where someone put on their skis and started skiing," RJ suggested as he pointed his flashlight at some ski tracks not far from the footprints.

"Maybe," Rebekah tilted her head from side to side as she considered it.

The next howl seemed to scream right over their heads. It was enough to get their attention again.

Rebekah ducked and looked up at the sky. "Whatever that is, I think we better find out where it's coming from, before it finds us."

"Good idea," RJ nodded.

Chapter 9

They began walking in the direction of the sound of the howling. As they walked toward the howling, all the leaves in the trees around them began shaking. They were rustling very loudly. It was a little strange. Rebekah pointed her flashlight up into the branches of the tree.

"What do you think is going on up there?" she asked with a frown.

"Probably just the wind," RJ shrugged and then shivered. "It's pretty cold when the wind blows!"

"I know, I wish we had worn ski masks," Rebekah shivered too and tightened the collar of her jacket around her neck. As Rebekah was speaking, they both saw a figure not far off. It was hard to tell just how far it was from them because it was so dark.

"Uh, do you think that's another snowman?" Rebekah asked in a whisper.

"Not this far from the lodge," RJ whispered back. As they were watching, the figure began to move toward them. They heard a loud shrill whistle.

"Ah!" Rebekah hid behind RJ at the strange sound.

"Even though I don't believe in ghosts," RJ said as calmly as he could. "I do think this might be a good time to run!"

Rebekah agreed with him, and they both began to run as fast as they could. The beams from their flashlights were bobbing up and down across the snow. It made the howling sound even spookier.

Finally, they had to slow down and catch their breath. Rebekah leaned on a nearby tree and peeked around it to see if the ghost, or whatever it was, was still behind them. She could hear the crunching, but she didn't see anything. What she also didn't see was the ski lodge.

"Uh, RJ?" Rebekah said in a whisper.

"What?" he gasped out as he was still trying to catch his breath.

"Do you know which way we're supposed to go to get back to the lodge?" she asked nervously.

"We just walk toward it," RJ said with a shrug. Then he looked in the direction Rebekah was looking. He only saw empty sky, trees and lots of snow. "Uh oh," he murmured. "Do you think we're lost?"

"We can't be lost," Rebekah said firmly. "Hey look," she pointed the flashlight toward the snow. "We can just follow our footprints back to the lodge."

"Good idea Rebekah," RJ said with a proud smile. "I never would have thought of that."

Chapter 10

As they followed their footsteps, they didn't hear the howling anymore. The trees weren't rustling so loudly either. It was actually pretty quiet. They had walked for a few minutes, when they suddenly heard the howling again.

"Eek!" Rebekah ducked behind the nearest tree. RJ ducked behind it too. The leaves in the tree were rustling quite loudly now, as if warning them to be careful.

"How are we ever going to get back to the ski lodge?" Rebekah whispered.

"Just wait, the howling stopped before, I'm sure it'll stop again," RJ whispered back. They waited for a few minutes as the howling got louder and louder. When the howling began to die down, they sighed with relief.

"Finally, let's get out of here," Rebekah said and started to step out from behind the tree. But before she could, they heard the crunching again. This time it was much louder. RJ pulled Rebekah back behind the tree.

"Stay back," he whispered. For once, RJ was a little scared.

"You know what, I'm not going to put up with this," Rebekah said with a frown and put her hands on her hips. "No ghost is going to scare me," she said sternly.

"What do you have in mind?" RJ asked as he looked at her curiously.

"I think we should scare the ghost first," Rebekah replied with a smile.

"Clever," RJ chuckled.

"Here get behind this tree," Rebekah instructed as she ducked down behind a large tree. RJ did the same and soon both of them were very well hidden by the thick trunk of the tree. They listened as the crunching drew closer to them. They could hear the howling still, though it didn't seem to be moving with the ghost.

"Wait for my signal," Rebekah whispered as they stayed crunched down.

"Okay, I think," RJ grinned as he peered around the side of the tree. He was still sure there was no such thing as ghosts, especially not a ghost snowman.

"Ready?" Rebekah whispered. "We're going to jump out and scare it when I say go, okay?"

"Okay," RJ nodded and got ready to jump out.

Chapter 11

"Go!" Rebekah shouted suddenly and jumped to her feet and out from behind the tree. RJ was right behind her. He roared and Rebekah shouted, "Boo!"

The figure before them let out a wild shriek. Then it slipped in the snow and started rolling down the ski slope. It wailed the whole time as it rolled down through the snow.

"Look at it go!" Rebekah gasped. "I can't believe we really scared a ghost!"

"I can't believe there really was a ghost," RJ said with wide eyes. "Hurry up, maybe we can catch it," he said.

He started running carefully down the slope. Rebekah followed after him, being very careful not to slip. When they reached the bottom of the slope they found what looked just like a snowman in a pile on the ground.

"Ugh," the snowman groaned. Rebekah and RJ stepped back a little. The snowman started to sit up. It dusted itself off and started to stand up.

"Uh oh," Rebekah whispered to RJ. "I don't think snowmen should be able to stand up and move around like that! Maybe we should run!"

"No!" the ghost snowman said sharply and started stumbling toward them. "No running! You two stay right there!" he grumbled and continued to dust himself off.

Chapter 12

As more and more of the snow was brushed off of his bulky jacket and ski pants, Rebekah and RJ began to realize that he wasn't a snowman at all. In fact, it wasn't a ghost either. It was Matt, their ski instructor!

"Matt!" Rebekah gasped and looked over at RJ who was just as surprised to see Matt.

"We didn't know it was you!" RJ frowned as Matt pulled off his ski mask and shook the snow off of it.

"Well I hope not," Matt growled. "Because I'm sure if you knew it was me, you wouldn't have shouted and made me roll all the way down that slope!" he said gruffly. He had his hands on his hips and didn't look too happy about being scared down the ski slope.

"What are you doing out here?" Rebekah asked with surprise.

"What am I doing out here?" Matt demanded. "What are you doing out here? I saw you two wandering around and I was worried that you would get lost, so I tried to catch up with you."

"We were looking for the ghost snowman," RJ explained with a sigh. "We didn't know it was you."

"You know kids, that story was meant to keep you from wandering around the ski slopes at night. Not to inspire you to wander around the ski slopes at night!" he shook his head as he pulled his ski mask back on. "What kind of kids would go hunting for a ghost instead of being scared of one?" he demanded.

"Well uh, we're not just kids," Rebekah explained with a grin. "We're detectives."

"The best detectives," RJ added. "We just wanted to solve the mystery."

"Well, you've solved it," Matt sighed. "There are no ghost snowmen. I just wanted to keep you safe. I guess I didn't do a very good job."

"Sure you did," Rebekah said with a smile. "RJ and I used the buddy system the whole time. We walked carefully on the slopes. We even made sure we brought our whistles," she showed him the whistle that was hanging around her neck.

"Well I guess the only one who wasn't safe was me," Matt laughed. "When I saw how windy and cold it was and heard all the howling of the wind through the mountains, I just didn't want you two to be out here alone. I even used my whistle to get your attention. But I'll admit, when you jumped out like that, it sure spooked me. That was one long roll down the hill," he added with a chuckle and a groan.

"It looked like fun," Rebekah said as they began walking back toward the ski lodge. "Was it fun?"

"I wouldn't recommend it," Matt laughed and shook his head. He led them back to the ski lodge. Rebekah was glad to get inside and get warm.

Even though it had been a little scary solving the mystery of the ghost snowman, she was glad that she had the chance to be a detective with RJ once again.

Rebekah - Girl Detective #14

Monkey Business

Chapter 1

Field trips were by far Rebekah's favorite part of school. It was a chance to be outside of the school with her friends and they always went to interesting places.

They were going to the zoo for their field trip and Rebekah was pretty excited. Her mother had given her a new camera to use on the trip because she wanted to see lots of pictures of the animals.

Mouse was excited too, mostly because they had a special exhibit of Malagasy Jumping Rats. Rebekah was a little unnerved at the idea of jumping rats, but she was excited because her best friend Mouse was excited.

At the top of Rebekah's list to see was a young monkey that had been born only a few weeks earlier. The zoo had made a big deal of welcoming the baby, and even held a contest to see who could name it.

It was a lot of fun to take part in the contest and Rebekah was eager to see what the monkey had been named.

On the bus ride to the zoo she and Mouse talked about the different animals they would see. Rebekah also played with her new camera. She was snapping a picture of Mouse when his pet mouse poked its head up out of his pocket.

"Oh no you brought a mouse?" Rebekah hissed so the teachers wouldn't hear.

"He didn't want to miss it!" Mouse said with a frown. "Don't worry it's just Gabe, he likes to be very quiet and hide in my pocket."

"I hope so," Rebekah frowned. "Because if he gets loose in the zoo it's going to be very hard to find him."

"I know," Mouse nodded.

Chapter 2

When they reached the zoo the teachers paired them up with buddies. Rebekah chose Mouse, of course, and they were off to see the animals.

As they walked through the zoo Rebekah was looking over a map that she had been handed at the entrance. She wanted to get to the monkey section as soon as she could, because she knew it would be very crowded.

Mouse was looking at a map too and he started walking in the opposite direction toward the rodent area.

"Stay together kids!" Mrs. Duncan called out from behind them. Her voice was very loud because she had brought along a bull horn. Rebekah and Mouse looked up at the same time to see that they were walking very far apart.

"Oops," Rebekah laughed as she walked over to Mouse. "I'm sorry I wanted to see the monkeys."

"Oh," Mouse frowned with disappointment. "I was hoping to see the Malagasy Jumping Rats first."

Rebekah frowned too. She really wanted to see the monkeys, but she knew that Mouse was excited about the rats.

"Okay we'll go see the rats first," Rebekah nodded. "But then you have to let me take a picture of you with the monkeys!"

"Alright, fine," Mouse grinned. As they hurried toward the rodent section of the zoo, Rebekah nearly bumped into a boy who was running in the opposite direction.

"Excuse me," Rebekah said as she stepped aside so that they wouldn't slam into each other.

"Sorry," he mumbled and hurried off. Rebekah noticed that he was carrying a bunch of bananas. It was a strange snack to bring to the zoo, but she only shrugged and followed after mouse.

While Mouse oohed and ahhed over the jumping rats, Rebekah snapped pictures of them and other animals nearby. She even got a picture of one of the teachers running from the lion cages.

It wasn't until Rebekah turned back around that she realized that Mouse was leaning very far over the side of the rat enclosure.

"Mouse!" Rebekah squeaked and ran over to him. She reached out just in time and caught Gabe before he could fall in.

"Oops," Mouse took Gabe from her and tucked him back into his pocket. "Sorry Rebekah," he grinned sheepishly.

"Just keep him in there," Rebekah said firmly. "Can we go see the monkeys now?" she asked hopefully.

"Sure," Mouse nodded. "Would you mind taking a picture of me with the rats?" he asked.

"No problem," Rebekah agreed. She took a few steps back and waited for one of the rats to jump. Then she took a picture of Mouse, with a rat over his shoulder and a mouse poking its head up out of his pocket. She had to admit it looked pretty funny.

She decided to take one more picture, but before she could the same boy who she had almost bumped into earlier, walked right in front of the camera. He had his jacket bundled up in his arms.

"Sorry, sorry," he said as he hurried through the picture. Rebekah was so surprised that she accidentally took the picture.

"One more," Rebekah sighed. Mouse was getting tired of smiling but he managed to hold it long enough for Rebekah to get another good picture. As they walked over to the monkeys, Rebekah was still a little annoyed.

"That boy was so rude," she said with a frown. "He didn't have to walk right in front of the camera. He could have walked around. Do you know him?" she asked.

"I think his name is Lucas," Mouse said with a shrug. "He's not in any of my classes, but I remember him from an assembly about animal rights. I went to it because of my mice, poor little guys are always being used as lab rats."

"I've never seen him before," Rebekah frowned. "He must not be in my classes either."

"Oh well, don't let it ruin our day," Mouse said with a smile. "Up next, a picture of Mouse with the monkeys!"

Rebekah laughed and followed after him to the monkey section of the zoo.

Chapter 3

Just as Rebekah had expected, the monkey section of the zoo was packed. It seemed like everybody wanted to see the littlest monkey at the zoo. As she and Mouse tried to get closer, Rebekah realized, the crowd was buzzing. But it wasn't because of the cute little monkey. It was because the monkey was missing.

"Where is he?" one of the teachers whispered to another.

"Could he have gotten loose?" one of the kids wondered. Rebekah noticed one of the zoo staff members standing beside the cage. He looked very sad. Rebekah and Mouse slipped over to him.

"Is the little monkey really missing?" Rebekah asked with a frown.

"Yes," the zookeeper sighed. "I just checked on him fifteen minutes ago and he was snuggled up to his Mom. Now he's gone!"

Rebekah frowned as she thought of the poor little monkey without its mother. She looked at all the kids and teachers that were bunched around the cages.

"Don't worry," she said with a smile. "We can all help you look!"

The zookeeper thought about it a moment and then nodded. "That's actually a very good idea," he said. The crowd was so noisy that it was hard to get their attention. So Rebekah found the teacher with the bull horn.

"Can you announce to everyone that the zookeeper has something to say?" she asked politely.

"I can do better than that," Mrs. Duncan said. "I can give him the bull horn."

She handed over the bull horn to the zookeeper and he turned it on.

"Excuse me!" he said, and looked a little startled by how loud his voice was. "Excuse me," he tried again, and soon all of the people in the crowd were quieting down. "I'd like to ask for your help," the zookeeper said calmly. "Our little monkey is missing. I don't know how he got out, but we need to find him.

Since there are so many of you here, I thought we could all search together." All of the people in the crowd shouted that they would help.

"We've never had an animal escape before and I want you to know that this monkey is not aggressive. He won't hurt you, but he might be very scared. So if you spot him, please don't pick him up just let one of the zoo staff know that you've found him," the zookeeper then began splitting up everyone in the crowd into smaller groups, each with a teacher to lead them.

Rebekah and Mouse were assigned to Mrs. Duncan who was beside herself with concern.

"Poor little monkey. We've got to find him. What if he wanders into one of tiger cages?" she sighed.

"Maybe we should check in the most dangerous spots first," Rebekah suggested. She really wanted to go off to search by herself, but she knew that she had to stay with the teacher. Rebekah was a very good detective and a missing monkey was a mystery she knew that she could solve. She just had to think it through.

Chapter 4

"Mrs. Duncan, what if the monkey didn't escape?" she asked thoughtfully. "What if someone took him?"

"Oh Rebekah I don't think that's what happened," Mrs. Duncan shook her head. "Who would steal a monkey?"

Rebekah frowned, but she didn't think she was wrong. It was the cage itself that made her think someone took the monkey.

The zookeeper said he had just checked on the monkey a few minutes before it went missing. Maybe he had left the door to the cage open? But when Rebekah had looked at the cage, it was all locked up.

She did notice from the picture of the monkey on the display that it was very tiny. Some of the bars on the monkey cage were a bit wider than the others. Maybe he had slipped out. But if he was snuggled up with his mother why would he want to leave the cage?

Rebekah waited until everyone had cleared out from in front of the cage.

"Mrs. Duncan, I need to use the bathroom," Rebekah said quickly.

"Alright Rebekah. Mouse you walk with her, you are her buddy," Mrs. Duncan said sternly. "And both of you meet us by the tiger cage, okay?"

"Yes Mrs. Duncan," Rebekah nodded. Mouse glanced over at Rebekah as Mrs. Duncan walked away.

"You don't really have to use the bathroom, do you?" he asked as he looked at her.

"No," Rebekah admitted. "I wanted to take a closer look at the cage."

"Do you really think someone took the monkey?" Mouse asked with surprise.

"It just doesn't make sense to me that he would escape," Rebekah said with a frown. "Don't you think someone would have seen him if he slipped through the bars?"

"You're right," Mouse nodded. "Everyone was there to see the little monkey, I'm sure they would have said something if he was sneaking out."

"Look at his," Rebekah said as she pointed out the lock on the door of the cage. "It's locked up tight. There's no way it was left open. But no one would have been able to break in either."

"Maybe someone had the key?" Mouse suggested.

"Maybe," Rebekah frowned. She noticed the zookeeper talking with a police officer that had been called to help aid in the search. "We should ask the zookeeper who has keys to the cages."

Chapter 5

They waited for the zookeeper to finish talking to the police officer, and then walked over to him.

"Excuse me sir, can I ask you a question?" Rebekah asked.

"Sure," he nodded, but he was very upset.

"Who has keys to the monkey cages?" Rebekah asked.

"Only me," the zookeeper sighed. "I'm the only one with the key. I know I locked the door," he added.

"And you're sure the monkey was there when you checked?" Rebekah asked with a frown.

"Yes I'm sure," the zookeeper nodded. "I noticed that his bowl was empty so I was going to get him some food. He was sleeping, and I knew when he woke up he would be hungry. I just don't know how this could happen," he said with a shake of his head. "I'm always so careful," he sighed as he walked away. Rebekah found it hard to believe that the zookeeper would be careless. He seemed to take his job very seriously. She suspected something else must have happened. But if no one else had the key, how could anyone have gotten the monkey out?

Rebekah peered through the bars of the monkey cage.

"Look at that," Rebekah said as she pointed to something inside the cage.

"What is it?" Mouse asked as she looked where she pointed.

"It looks like a banana peel," Rebekah said with narrowed eyes.

"Well monkeys do like bananas," Mouse reminded her with a shrug.

"But the zookeeper said he had been going to get food for the little monkey," Rebekah explained. "He said the bowl was empty. That banana peel looks fresh. So where did it come from?" she asked.

"That is odd," Mouse agreed. Rebekah decided to get a closer look at the peel. She couldn't get inside the cage, but she could zoom in with her camera. She did just that and snapped a picture. As she studied the picture on the back of her camera she nodded.

"It's definitely a banana peel and it's bright yellow so there's no way it's been sitting in there for very long," she said firmly. "No Mouse, I don't think this little monkey escaped. I think someone helped him out of the cage."

"But how?" Mouse asked. "There's a roof on the cage."

"Well these bars are further apart than the others," Rebekah pointed out as she measured the distance between the bars with her fingers. "That monkey is very little and he probably could squeeze through here."

"But remember, people were watching," Mouse said with a frown.

"Good point," Rebekah sighed and shook her head. "This is a tough one."

"Let's think it through," Mouse said. "If you think that someone stole the monkey, then you probably think someone gave him the banana."

"A banana!" Rebekah snapped her fingers. "Remember that boy? He had a whole bunch of bananas!"

"Oh that's right," Mouse nodded. "But that doesn't mean he's the one who gave the monkey the banana."

"No it doesn't," Rebekah agreed. "But there was something else odd too," she said quietly. "Remember when he walked through the picture of you with the rats?" she began flipping through the camera. "When I saw him with the bananas the first time, he was wearing his jacket. When he walked through the picture he was carrying it," Rebekah recalled.

"Well it did get a bit warmer out," Mouse pointed out.

Chapter 6

"Hm," Rebekah looked down at the picture she had accidentally snapped of the boy. She made it larger on the screen. As she did her eyes widened. "Uh Mouse," she showed him the picture. "That jacket has a tail!"

"Oh wow!" Mouse gasped as he saw the brown tail sticking out from the end of the jacket. "You're right Rebekah. Do you think he's really the one who stole the monkey?"

"Think about it," Rebekah said in a whisper. "The monkey woke up hungry and Lucas had bananas. He probably tossed the monkey one of the bananas. Then when the monkey wanted more, he took off his jacket. He could have laid it against the bars so that no one would see the monkey slipping through the bars to reach for another banana!"

"Wow," Mouse shook his head. "I wouldn't think a kid could do this," he frowned as he glanced over at the police officer who was interviewing some of the people who had been standing beside the monkey's cage. "Lucas isn't a bad kid Rebekah, but if he gets caught, he's going to be in big trouble."

"I know," Rebekah said with a frown as she glanced up at the officer too. "That's why we've got to find him before anyone else does."

Mouse glanced at his watch. "If we don't get back to Mrs. Duncan, we're going to be the ones in big trouble."

"Good point," Rebekah frowned. "Let's see if we can find out which group Lucas is supposed to be in," she suggested.

As they walked off to rejoin Mrs. Duncan and the rest of their group Rebekah saw all of the kids, teachers and other zoo visitors searching for the monkey. She knew that she should tell the zookeeper about the picture she had, but she didn't want to get Lucas into too much trouble.

If they could just find him, maybe they could convince him to give the monkey back. Rebekah glanced over her shoulder at the monkey cage and saw the little monkey's mother looking sadly through the bars.

"We have to find Lucas," she said firmly.

Chapter 7

"Oh good, there you two are," Mrs. Duncan said with a sigh. "What took you so long?"

"We thought we saw the monkey in a tree," Rebekah explained with a shrug. "Sorry."

"It's okay, it's just that they have shut all of the exits of the zoo and I wanted to make sure you two were safe," Mrs. Duncan explained.

"So no one is able to leave the zoo?" Rebekah asked with surprise.

"No, they're afraid the little monkey might escape through one of the exits, so they have it all locked up!" she glanced around at the other animal cages around them. "I just hope they find him soon, this wasn't exactly what we had planned for our field trip."

"Well we better start looking," Rebekah said. "Maybe we should check the elephant enclosure," she suggested. "That's very open and the monkey could hop right in."

"Good idea," Mrs. Duncan nodded and started to lead the kids toward the elephant enclosure.

"Very clever," Mouse whispered to her. "The elephant enclosure is all the way at the back of the zoo so we'll have to walk past all of the other groups to get to it."

"Exactly," Rebekah nodded. "So keep your eyes peeled."

"I will," Mouse promised. "Lucas couldn't have gotten too far, and that monkey isn't going to stay hidden in his jacket for too long."

As they walked, several of the zoo staff members were checking all of the animal cages. They checked everything from the giraffes, to the bird sanctuary, to the crocodile cage. But they all came back out with a frown and no monkey.

Rebekah knew how badly the zookeeper felt for the baby monkey going missing. Everyone seemed to think it was his fault and only Rebekah, Mouse and Lucas knew that it wasn't.

Chapter 8

"There!" Mouse pointed to a group that was gathered beside a glass enclosure filled with porcupines. "I think that's him," Mouse whispered to Rebekah.

Rebekah saw a boy standing at the back of the group. He had his jacket on, but he had it on backwards. It was odd to see, but no one else seemed to notice it.

"It is him," Rebekah hissed as she pointed to a brown tail that was sticking out of the bottom of Lucas' jacket.

"Hurry we have to get to him," Rebekah said as she and Mouse started to break away from their group.

"Where are you going?" Mrs. Duncan asked from right behind them. "I told you two to stay close."

Rebekah frowned as she turned to face Mrs. Duncan. "I'm sorry, we thought we saw something by the porcupines."

"Mr. Tuttle's group is looking over there," Mrs. Duncan said firmly. "Please we already have a missing monkey, I don't want to have a missing Mouse or a missing Rebekah!"

"Sorry Mrs. Duncan," Mouse said and shoved his hands in his pockets. When Mrs. Duncan walked back to the front of the group, Rebekah's eyes widened.

"That's it! A missing mouse!" she said as she looked at Mouse.

"Huh?" Mouse asked.

"You're going to have to distract everyone. Actually, Gabe is going to have to distract everyone," she said and pointed to the mouse hiding in his pocket.

"Oh but Rebekah like you said the zoo is so big and-" Mouse frowned.

"Don't worry," Rebekah promised him. "We'll make sure he's safe. I'll go on one side of the path, and you go on the other. Let Gabe run across and scare everyone, then I'll catch him."

"Alright," Mouse finally nodded.

Chapter 9

They hung back a few steps behind their group. Then Mouse let his pet free on one side of the path.

"Eek! Mouse!" Rebekah cried out as the little white blur bolted across the path.

"Mouse?" Mrs. Duncan asked, thinking that Rebekah was talking about her friend. Then she saw the white blur.

"Mouse!" she shrieked. Rebekah reached down to catch Gabe, but Gabe was scared of her. He was a very timid mouse and he ran in the other direction. He ran right into the elephant cage! All of the elephants started trumpeting and stomping when they saw the mouse in their enclosure.

Mouse gasped. "Gabe!" he cried out. Rebekah felt horrible. She had promised Mouse that his pet would be safe.

She spotted Lucas looking over at the commotion. All of the groups were gathering together to see what all of the shrieking was about. Rebekah knew that if she didn't catch Lucas now he might get away, but she had promised Mouse that Gabe wouldn't get lost.

She turned back in time to see the little white mouse bolt right out of the other side of the elephant cage.

"Come on Mouse!" she called out and they ran after Gabe. Mouse almost had him, when he slipped into the enclosure with the jumping rats. The rats started going wild, jumping everywhere.

"Oh no!" Mouse slapped his forehead. "We're never going to get him out of there," he groaned.

"Sure we will," Rebekah said sternly. She glanced in one direction, and then in the other. Everyone was busy looking for the monkey. No one was looking at the jumping rat cage.

She handed Mouse her bag and camera and then jumped right into the cage.

"Rebekah!" Mouse gasped and nearly dropped her camera. He accidentally took a picture of Rebekah surrounded by jumping rats.

"Do you see him?" Rebekah asked as the rats jumped all around her. She had to duck when one tried to land on her head.

Mouse looked down at the picture he had taken and spotted Gabe in the corner of the cage.

"In the corner!" he called to Rebekah. "Hurry before he gets away!"

Rebekah caught Gabe in her hands and carried him back to Mouse. Mouse tucked him safely into his pocket and then helped Rebekah out of the cage.

"Thank you so much Rebekah!" Mouse sighed with relief.

"I promised to keep him safe," Rebekah frowned. "Too bad we can't do the same for the little monkey. I bet Lucas is long gone by now."

Chapter 10

"That was very brave Rebekah," Lucas said from beside her.

"Lucas?" Rebekah gasped as she looked at him.

"I saw what you did," Lucas said as he hugged his jacket that was hiding the little monkey. "You must really love animals like I do."

"Well, it was Mouse's pet," Rebekah explained as she looked at the tail swishing at the bottom of his jacket. "Just like that little monkey is his mother's baby," she said softly.

"But he shouldn't be in a cage Rebekah," Lucas said sternly. "The animals should get to live free, in the wild where they belong."

"But Lucas, how is he going to survive without his mom to teach him how to?" Rebekah asked. She didn't want to make him angry and have him run off. "I know that you want to protect the little monkey, but so does the monkey's mom."

"I don't know," Lucas frowned. "I think he needs to be free. I can take care of him."

"Oh Lucas, you can't have a monkey as a pet," Mouse said with a shake of his head. "Monkeys need a lot of care. Maybe being in the zoo isn't the best place for him, but it's where his family is, and they will take very good care of him."

"How do you know?" Lucas asked.

"Look," Rebekah pointed to the zookeeper who was sitting on a bench with his head in his hands. "Look how upset he is that the monkey is missing. He really cares about the animals he takes care of."

"I guess you're right," Lucas frowned. "But what can I do now? If I tell the truth, I'm going to get in a lot of trouble."

"That's for sure," Mouse nodded as he noticed a few more police officers had entered the zoo.

"Well maybe we can put the monkey back instead," Rebekah suggested. "If you could sneak him out, we can sneak him back in!"

"But everyone is looking for him now," Mouse reminded Rebekah.

"We can do it," Rebekah promised. "Let's give it a try."

Chapter 11

Since the monkey cage had been searched so well when the little monkey first went missing, there weren't too many people around it. But Mrs. Duncan was looking for Rebekah and Mouse, so they had to be careful.

They walked behind the cages and hid behind trees as they crept toward the monkey cage. The little monkey was getting restless under Lucas' jacket. He kept whipping Lucas with his tail.

"Shh," Lucas pleaded with the monkey.

"It's okay, he just wants his mother," Rebekah said sadly. "Look, she's waiting for him," Rebekah said and pointed to the monkey cage. The little monkey's mother was standing class to the bars and seemed to be looking for the monkey.

"It's now or never," Lucas sighed. "I guess I didn't think this through."

"You wanted to protect him," Mouse shrugged. "I know what that's like. But now he needs to go back to his mother."

Lucas took a deep breath and began walking across the path to the monkey cage. Rebekah and Mouse followed close behind him. Just like Lucas had done before, he took off his jacket and used it to hide the monkey.

The little monkey held his breath and squeezed through the bars of the cage. His mother was waiting for him on the other side.

"Rebekah? Mouse?" Mrs. Duncan was calling as she walked toward the cage.

"Lucas, go back to your group," Rebekah said in a whisper. "That way no one will know you were here."

"Are you sure?" Lucas asked with a frown.

"You did the right thing," Mouse nodded. "Just blend in and ditch the rest of those bananas, huh?" Mouse pointed out the bananas that Lucas still had in his pocket.

"Okay," Lucas nodded. He tossed them into the monkey cage before running off to the group he was supposed to be with.

"Rebekah and Mouse," Mrs. Duncan said from right behind them. "You're both in big trouble. I told you to stay with the group!"

"We were," Rebekah said with wide eyes. "But then we saw this and had to look closer to make sure we were right!" Rebekah explained.

Chapter 12

"Saw what?" Mrs. Duncan asked as she looked where Rebekah was pointing. The little monkey was wrapped up in his mother's arms.

"Oh the monkey!" Mrs. Duncan cried out getting everyone's attention. "The monkey is back!"

The zookeeper came running back over. He couldn't believe his eyes.

"But I searched that cage myself!" he said. Once all of the cheering had died down, Rebekah pulled the zookeeper aside and spoke in a whisper to him.

"You might want to check the bars on the cage," she said. "That's one skinny monkey."

The zookeeper looked right at her. "I know that monkey was not in the cage," he said with a frown. "You and your friend had something to do with this, didn't you?"

Rebekah looked at him nervously. She wondered if he was going to be upset.

When she didn't answer, he just smiled. "Look I don't know how you did it, but I'm happy you did. In fact, I'm so happy, I want you to be the one to name the monkey. We haven't picked a winner yet."

"Really?" Rebekah asked with surprise.

"Sure, can you think of a good name for him?" he asked. Rebekah looked over at Mouse who had Gabe in his hand and was talking softly to him about the monkeys in the cage.

"Mouse!" she said with a laugh.

"Mouse?" the zookeeper raised an eyebrow. "A monkey named mouse is a little strange, but alright!"

Chapter 13

All the way home on the bus the kids talked about the newest little monkey at the zoo, a monkey named Mouse.

When Rebekah got home, her mother was very excited to see the pictures from the zoo.

"I didn't get too many," Rebekah frowned as she handed over the camera. She was tired from the exciting day, so she headed to her room for a rest. Rebekah's mother began looking through the pictures on the camera. Rebekah had just lay down on her bed when she hear her mother gasp.

"Rebekah!" she shouted. Rebekah sat bolt upright in bed, her eyes wide.

"Yes?" she asked as she ran out to the living room.

"Can you explain why you were inside a cage of jumping rats?" her mother asked as she tapped her foot and held out the camera.

Rebekah gulped as she looked at the picture of all the rats jumping around her.

"Uh, that's kind of a long story Mom," Rebekah said with a laugh.

"Good, we've got plenty of time," her mother said and sat down on the couch. She patted cushion beside her. "I want to hear all about it."

"Did you know I got to name a monkey after Mouse?" Rebekah asked as she tried to change the subject.

"Next time there's a field trip to the zoo, I'm going to chaperone," her mother shook her head as she looked through the rest of the pictures. "Does that boy have a tail?" she asked as she tilted the camera to the side.

"Well uh, that's a longer story," Rebekah laughed and shook her head. She was glad to have solved the mystery of the missing monkey, but she was a little worried about whether her mother might decide to do some detective work of her own.

Rebekah - Girl Detective #15
Science Magic

Chapter 1

One of Rebekah's favorite classes was science. Not just because of the subject, but because of the teacher. Rebekah had a few science teachers in the past that were pretty great. But by far her favorite was her current science teacher, Mr. Woods.

He was always thinking up new ways to teach them fun science concepts. Rebekah looked forward to his class because she saw science as just another mystery to solve.

One day Rebekah walked into Mr. Woods' class to see something very surprising. In the middle of his desk was a strange cylinder. In the middle of the cylinder a small square magnet was floating in midair!

"Wow!" Rebekah said as she looked at it closely. "How is that happening?" she wondered.

"Magic!" Mr. Woods said as he stepped up behind his desk.

"Oh Mr. Woods I don't believe in magic," Rebekah shook her head. As a detective, she had solved many mysteries. Some of them looked pretty magical at the start, but they always ended up being something much simpler than she expected.

"Well, this is science magic," Mr. Woods explained with a grin. "Look," he opened a small door on the plastic cylinder and poked his finger against the magnet. It moved, but it still floated. "See?" he said. "No strings."

'Wow," Rebekah said with wide eyes.

"Oh that old trick," Max laughed as he walked into class. Max was one of Rebekah's friends. His father was a scientist, so science was his favorite class.

"Don't tell Max!" Mr. Woods warned him. "I want Rebekah to figure it out."

"Oh she will," Max laughed. "Rebekah can figure anything out!"

Rebekah smiled at Max, then she looked back at the floating magnet. As the other students filed into the class, Rebekah continued to stare. No matter how much she thought about it, she couldn't figure out how the magnet could be floating in midair the way it was. It was really beginning to bug her.

Chapter 2

"Alright class, today we have a special assignment," Mr. Woods said as he sat on the edge of his desk. "This is what I call science magic," he said as he pointed to the cylinder. "Did you figure it out yet Rebekah?" he asked as he looked over at her.

"I think so," Rebekah said thoughtfully.

"Well, why don't you tell us how you think it's done?" he asked with a smile.

"It's a trick," she said.

"No it's not a trick," Mr. Woods said firmly. "A trick is an illusion. This isn't an illusion. This magnet is really floating."

"Well there must be some kind of trick," one of the other kids called out. "Is there a fan or something?"

"No, no, fan," Mr. Woods said. "But that's a good thought."

"Rebekah, what do you think?" he asked and looked back at Rebekah.

"Well I know that magnets can push each other apart," Rebekah said with a frown. "Does it have something to do with that?"

"Absolutely," Mr. Woods said with a smile. "We have some special, powerful magnets here. See this one on top is a ceramic magnet," he explained as he pointed to the magnet at the top of the cylinder. "This one on the bottom is a magnet as well. They are repelling each other. The magnet in the middle is caught in the middle of their little fight," he grinned. "That's the easiest way to explain it."

"That's pretty amazing," Rebekah said with wide eyes.

"Yes it is," Mr. Woods said with a nod. "Science is pretty amazing. Sometimes we forget that science is a study that is constantly changing and growing. People are always discovering something new about our world and the laws of nature and science."

"Like scientists," Rebekah pointed out.

"No, not just scientists," Mr. Woods corrected her. "Some of the greatest discoveries have been made by average people, who stumbled on to a great idea.

That's what our assignment today is about. I'm not going to give you a set of directions. I'm going to ask you to come up with an amazing new idea. Then I want you to make it work. No volcanoes, or potato electricity," he said firmly. "Something new that you think of yourself. It really doesn't matter if it works. I just want to see what ideas you can come up with."

Rebekah liked the assignment already. It was like a mystery that she could solve. What new idea could she think of?

"Oh what's the point?" Bethany, another girl in the class grumbled from her desk behind Max. "It's not like any of us have a chance with Max in our class."

"Hey," Max frowned as he glanced over his shoulder. "That's not very nice."

"But it's true," Bethany crossed her arms. "No one is going to think of a better project than you."

"Let's all do our best," Mr. Woods said as the bell rang. Max glared at Bethany. Bethany glared back at Max. Rebekah frowned. Bethany was very good at science too, but she was always competing with Max in class.

"I'm sure we'll all come up with something," she said, hoping to cool off the tension between her friends.

Chapter 3

After class Rebekah was still thinking about the project she would create. She was very excited about the idea. She met her friend Mouse in the hallway by her locker.

"Guess what? Mr. Woods has a great assignment!" Rebekah said happily.

"I've heard," Mouse said happily. "Did you see the magnet trick? We could use that in a prank!" he laughed. Rebekah nodded.

"I bet we could," she grinned. Mouse had his own secret club that thought up great pranks that they could pull on people.

"I'm trying to think of a great idea," Rebekah said with a frown. "But it's harder than I thought!"

"Don't worry, you'll think of something," Mouse promised her.

By the time school was over that day Rebekah still couldn't think of anything. Any idea she came up with had already been done. She wanted something different, something that would showcase her talents as a detective. As she was putting her books away at the end of the day, Max walked up to her locker.

"Hey do you have an idea yet?" Max asked with a grin.

"Not yet," Rebekah frowned. "Do you?"

"Oh yeah, I've got a great one!" Max smirked. "But it's a secret."

"A secret huh?" Rebekah smiled.

"No detective work Rebekah!" he warned her with a wag of his finger.

"No way," she promised. "I'm too busy thinking of my project, to figure out yours!"

"Well Mr. Woods said we have a week, so that will give you plenty of time," Max smiled. "Good luck!"

Chapter 4

Rebekah spent the whole week trying to come up with an idea. By the time Thursday night came around, she still didn't have a clue what to do. She was very disappointed. She decided to call Max to see if he could help her.

"Rebekah, I'm not telling you about my project," Max said as soon as he answered the phone.

"I was just hoping you might have an idea for me," Rebekah sighed. "I can't think of a single thing."

"Well you can always stick a carnation in a glass of water with food dye," he said with a laugh in his voice. "That's an easy project."

"Thanks a lot Max," she said with a sigh. She knew it was a simple project, but at least she would have something to turn in. "How is your project coming along?"

"It's great!" Max said enthusiastically. "I can't wait to show everyone tomorrow."

"Can't wait to see it," Rebekah said happily. She hung up the phone and went to look for her mother.

"Mom, do you know where we can buy a carnation and some food dye?" Rebekah asked just as her mother was sitting down to read her new book.

"Oh dear, do we need it now?" she asked.

"I need it by tomorrow morning," Rebekah cringed.

"Oh Rebekah," her mother shook her head.

"Sorry Mom," Rebekah smiled innocently.

When they reached the store, Rebekah hurried to pick out a flower. She spotted Bethany not far off. She had several bottles of paint, glue, and even some large Styrofoam balls in her arms.

"Hi Bethany," Rebekah said as she picked her flower. "Do you need some help?"

"No thanks," Bethany said with a frown. "No peeking at my project!"

"Okay, okay, sorry," Rebekah smiled. Bethany did not smile back. She walked right to the check-out lane. Rebekah was going to be glad when the assignment was over.

When she got home she put her flower in water with bright pink food coloring. Then she went to bed.

When she woke up the next day, her white carnation was bright pink.

"Well at least it worked," she shrugged. She stuck the carnation in a plastic zip-lock bag and tucked it into her bag. She was excited about seeing both Max and Bethany's projects.

Chapter 5

When she got to school she found Max standing beside his locker.

"Ready to turn in your project?" Rebekah asked from just behind him, causing him to jump.

"No peeking Rebekah!" Max growled and closed his locker.

"I wasn't peeking," Rebekah said as she rolled her eyes. "This project has turned you and Bethany into monsters!"

"Science monsters," Max wiggled his eyebrows.

"See you at class," Rebekah laughed. After her first class Rebekah stepped out into the hall. She was greeted by a loud scream.

"Someone stole my project!" Max frowned as he looked in his locker. "I put it in here this morning, and it's not here now!"

"Are you sure someone took it?" Rebekah asked. "Maybe you misplaced it?"

"I didn't," Max said firmly. "I put it right here to keep it safe until science class. Someone took it!"

He turned around and found Bethany standing not far from his locker. "Was it you?" he asked her with a glare.

"No!" Bethany gasped and shook her head. "It wasn't me."

"I know you were jealous about my project," Max argued with frustration. "Did you take it so that Mr. Woods would like your project best?"

"No, I didn't," Bethany said with tears in her eyes. "I didn't, I really didn't Max."

Rebekah frowned as she put an arm around Bethany's shoulders. "It's okay, don't get upset she said."

"She should be upset," Max huffed. "She took my project. I know she's the one who did it."

"But I didn't," Bethany argued and sniffled. "You have to believe me Rebekah."

Rebekah frowned. She and Max were good friends, but she had never known Bethany to steal anything. Sure she had been determined to create a better project than Max, but that didn't mean she would do something as terrible as stealing it. But if she didn't take Max's project, then who did?

"We'll see what Mr. Woods has to say about it," Max said firmly and started walking off toward the science classroom.

"Oh no, now Mr. Woods is going to think I'm a thief too," Bethany sighed. "You know I didn't do it, don't you Rebekah?" she asked hopefully.

"Sure I do," Rebekah said quietly. "Don't worry about Max, he's just upset. Mr. Woods won't believe him. Especially if I figure out what really happened to Max's project."

"Oh I hope you do," Bethany said and sniffled again. "I don't want Max to be angry with me."

Chapter 6

Rebekah found Max heading for the principal's office to report Bethany.

"Max wait," Rebekah said as she chased after him. Mouse caught up with them too, as he wondered what all the shouting was about. "Maybe it wasn't Bethany," Rebekah said. "Why don't you let me try to figure out what happened?"

"Alright," Max nodded. "If anyone can figure it out, it's you Rebekah," he sighed. "But I'm sure it was Bethany."

"Listen, in order for me to figure it out, you're going to have to tell me what your project looked like," Rebekah said.

"It was goo," Mouse admitted. "Bright green goo. That should be hard to hide."

"Okay, we're going to find it, aren't we Mouse?" she glanced over at Mouse who was petting the top of the head of a mouse in his top shirt pocket.

"Yes, we will," he said with a nod.

"We'll have to start with your locker," Rebekah said.

Max wrote down the combination for her. "I hope you can find it," he said with a frown as he walked off to his next class.

Rebekah and Mouse hurried to Max's locker. Rebekah unlocked it and opened it up. Inside it was pretty empty. But it had a strange smell. It wasn't a bad smell, like when Mouse left pieces of cheese for his mice in his locker for too long. It was a sharp smell, like lemon.

"Weird, Max doesn't smell like lemon," Rebekah said as she sniffed the locker.

"What does Max smell like?" Mouse laughed.

"I'm not sure, but it's not lemon," Rebekah giggled. Then she looked more closely at the door of the locker. She crouched down and looked at the bottom to see if it might have been pried open. It wasn't, but there was a bit of green goop on it.

"Hm," Rebekah said as she rubbed the goop between her fingers. "We have green goo," she said and looked up at Mouse with a grin.

"Gross," Mouse shivered a little.

"Well if no one broke into Max's locker, then someone must have had another way to get in," Rebekah said thoughtfully. "Or maybe," she looked at the small air vents on the front of the locker. "Maybe someone got that strong vacuum they used to vacuum up that overflow in the boys room. If they put the hose up to the air vent, maybe they vacuumed the goo right out!"

"Who would do that?" Mouse said with a frown.

"I don't know, but it's a place to start," Rebekah suggested. Just then the bell rang.

"Meet me near the janitor's closet when class is over," Rebekah said quickly.

Chapter 7

Her next class was with Bethany. She noticed that Bethany looked very sad as they read a story in English class. She had a big bag beside her desk. Rebekah thought it probably had her science project in it.

Rebekah looked closely, but she didn't see any green goo on the bag. As soon as class was over, Rebekah waited for Bethany to leave. Then she looked over her desk closely for any traces of goo.

She didn't find anything at all, but she did smell something familiar. It was a sharp scent. It smelled like lemon. Rebekah's eyes widened. She didn't think that Bethany had taken Max's project, but why did her desk smell like Max's locker?

She hoped she wasn't wrong about Bethany. When she met Mouse beside the janitor's closet he looked a little nervous.

"I was thinking about something Rebekah," he said as she opened the door to the janitor's closet. "When you said someone could have used the vacuum to suck the goo out of the locker, it reminded me of something else that is good at sucking."

"What?" Rebekah asked as she ducked inside the closet. She found the vacuum pretty fast because it was pretty big.

"Like a vampire!" Mouse said as he kept watch for her.

"That's ridiculous Mouse," Rebekah rolled her eyes. She picked up the hose attached to the vacuum. "Aha!" she said. "Look," she stuck her finger inside the opening of the hose and came out with her finger tip covered in green goo. "I was right!"

"That doesn't mean it wasn't a vampire," Mouse pointed out.

"It's not a vampire Mouse," Rebekah said firmly. "But now we have to figure out who used the vacuum."

"Well it wasn't the janitor," Mouse said. "Remember Mr. Hugh retired last week."

"Good point," Rebekah nodded. Mr. Hugh was the janitor at the school but the teachers had a party for him to celebrate his retirement. So there shouldn't have been a janitor to use the vacuum. "Whoever used this vacuum took Max's science project," she said with certainty. As she stood up she caught a whiff of that strong lemon scent again. She sniffed until she found where it was coming from.

"Look at this Mouse," Rebekah said as she showed him a bottle of lemon scented cleaner. "This is what I smelled in Max's locker. I also smelled it at Bethany's desk. Maybe she really did take his project. If she came in here for the vacuum, she might have spilled some on herself."

"Who's there?" A voice bellowed from the shadows in the back of the closet. "No kids should be in here! I'm warning you! It's very dangerous!"

Mouse and Rebekah looked at each other, and then ran out of the closet. They ran all the way to their next class.

"See, I told you it was a vampire!" Mouse said with a gasp. "Someone living in the shadows, someone dangerous," he added.

"It can't be," Rebekah rolled her eyes. "Meet me outside the cafeteria after lunch."

"I'll be there," Mouse promised. "Watch out for vampires!"

Chapter 8

During her next class Rebekah tried to think of different ideas. She was pretty sure it hadn't been Bethany, even though some of the evidence pointed to her. Whatever had yelled at them from the back of the janitor's closet, certainly hadn't been Bethany.

Once she had scratched Bethany off of her suspect list, she was back at square one for suspects.

She pulled out her notebook and stared down at a blank page of paper. Since she had no other good ideas, she scribbled: Green Goo Eating Vampire. She knew it was a silly idea, but at least it was an idea.

Then she thought about Max some more. Everyone knew Max was the best science student in the school. She was sure his project would have been the best in the class. Maybe someone wanted the project. Maybe someone like an evil scientist, or someone who worked for an evil science spy agency.

She arched an eyebrow and jotted down her idea. It made about as much sense as a goo eating vampire. She sighed as she realized neither idea was going to solve the mystery.

If she didn't figure out who had really taken Max's project, he might stay mad at Bethany. He might even turn her in to the principal. Rebekah hated to think of Bethany getting into trouble for something that she didn't do. She was determined to figure it out, and hopefully before science class.

At lunch time Rebekah was waiting for Mouse outside of the cafeteria. Most of the other kids were already out of the hallway. She was waiting in a small hallway that led to the bathrooms. It was the only place the lunch monitor wouldn't spot her. The hallway was pretty dark.

When she started hearing heavy footsteps walking toward her she was surprised. She glanced over her shoulder, but she didn't see anyone behind her. Then she heard the footsteps again. Rebekah looked over her shoulder again. She still didn't see anyone. But she did smell something. Lemon! Rebekah gasped and turned back just in time to find Mouse standing right in front of her.

"Are you okay?" Mouse asked when he saw her wide eyes.

"He's here," she whispered to him and pulled him behind the open girls' bathroom door. They both watched as a man with his head down trudged slowly past the bathroom. He had thick boots on. He reached down and wiped a paper towel over one of them. When he pulled the paper towel away, Rebekah had to cover her mouth to keep quiet. There was green goo on the paper towel!

He grumbled and tossed the towel into a trash can. Then he started trudging down the hall again.

"See, vampire," Mouse whispered. "What kind of person walks like that?"

Rebekah watched as the man seemed to be struggling to pull his feet off the floor with every step he took. It was rather odd.

"Well let's find out," Rebekah said sternly. "Come with me!" she said.

Chapter 9

They followed the man down the hall. When he opened the door to the janitor's closet, Rebekah and Mouse looked at each other.

"One, two, three!" Rebekah counted down. Then both Mouse and Rebekah shoved the man from behind. They were going to trap him in the closet. But when they tried to close the door, it was stuck. It wouldn't budge. They heard groaning from the back of the closet. Rebekah pulled out a penlight and shined it into the closet. She shined it right at the shadow of the man in the back of the closet.

"Who are you and what have you done with Max's goo?" Rebekah asked as she shined the flashlight right into the man's face.

"Hey, stop that!" he grumbled and pushed the flashlight away. "That hurts my eyes."

"See I told you he's a goo eating vampire," Mouse whispered beside Rebekah's ear.

"I'm not a vampire!" the man said and shook his head. He pushed his way out of the closet. "You kids are acting up. I'm going to tell the principal."

"Wait a minute, what kind of criminal tells the principal?" Rebekah asked with a frown.

"I'm not a criminal, I'm the janitor," the man said with a frown. "My name is Mr. Potter and it's my first day. Some first day," he added gruffly. "First I get sticky goo stuck to my shoes, then I have to clean all the desks in the English classroom because somebody sprayed silly string, and now I get shoved into a closet by a couple of kids," he shook his head.

"Oh," Rebekah's eyes widened as she realized the mistake they had made. "Sorry about the whole shoving you in the closet thing," Rebekah said with a sheepish smile.

"Why did you do it?" Mr. Potter asked with a glare. "Is it just because you kids like to pick on janitors?"

"No way!" Mouse shook his head.

"That's not it at all," Rebekah frowned. "Someone stole our friend Max's science project, and we thought it was you. We thought you might be a spy from some secret science agency," she explained calmly.

"Actually, I thought you were a goo eating vampire," Mouse pointed out.

"Some imaginations you kids have," Mr. Potter shook his head. "I didn't steal any science project. I'm not a spy for any science agency, and I'm no kind of vampire!"

"Sorry, but you did have some of Max's goo on your shoe," Rebekah pointed to the man's goo covered shoe.

"Oh that?" Mr. Potter shook his head. "Look, I wanted to make a good impression. I was walking down the hallway this morning, and I almost slipped and fell in a puddle of this green stuff," he sighed. "So I cleaned it up, but a few seconds later there was a new puddle!

That's when I realized it was leaking out of the bottom of one of the lockers. So I opened up the locker and cleaned it up," he explained. "There was some glass on the bottom of the locker too, so I cleaned that up too."

"Oh," Rebekah's eyes widened. "That must be what happened!"

Chapter 10

Just as she was about to tell Mouse her suspicion, the bell rang.

"Get to class kids, so you don't get in trouble," Mr. Potter said with a grave frown. "We'll just keep this little mishap between us."

"Thanks," Rebekah said with relief. She didn't want to have to deal with a trip to the principal when she had finally figured out the mystery! She waved to Mouse who hurried to his class while Rebekah headed for Mr. Woods' class. When she ducked inside Max was standing in front of Mr. Woods' desk with a frown.

"I don't have a project to turn in," Max said sadly.

"Well to be honest Max I'm very disappointed," Mr. Woods said with a shake of his head. "Out of all the kids in this class I expected you would at least turn in the assignment."

"I tried Mr. Woods, but someone stole it!" Max said and glowered over his shoulder at Bethany.

Bethany looked down and frowned. She pulled the big plastic garbage bag beside her closer to her desk.

"No max, no one stole it!" Rebekah said as she walked up behind Max. She was out of breath from practically running to class.

"What?" Max asked with surprise.

"Your green goo, was it in a glass container?" she asked.

"Yes, a glass beaker I brought from home," Max nodded.

"Well, I think that somehow the glass must have broken, and all the green goo was seeping out of the bottom of your locker. Mr. Potter the new janitor saw it and cleaned it all up. That's why you thought it was stolen!"

"Oh," Max said softly. "I was experimenting with combining some different chemicals to make super goo, maybe they caused the goo to expand so much they broke the glass."

"That would have been some interesting super goo," Mr. Woods said with a smile. "Alright Max, it's clear to me that you did do the assignment, so I will give you credit for it," Mr. Woods smiled.

"Thanks," Max said sadly. Then he turned around and walked over to Bethany. "I'm sorry I accused you Bethany."

"It's okay," Bethany said. "I'm sorry I acted so jealous. That super goo sounds like it would have been pretty great."

"Thanks," Max said, I guess I need to work on it a little more though.

"Maybe you should use plastic instead of glass," Bethany suggested. "Like a plastic bag, that way it can expand if the goo expands."

"What a great idea!" Max grinned. "Want to come over after school and try it out?"

"I would love to!" Bethany said happily. "Want to see my project?" she asked with a smile.

"Yes please," Max nodded.

Chapter 11

Bethany carried the bag up to the front desk. She opened it up and placed the objects on the desk. "Remember when someone mentioned a fan in class?" she said. "It gave me an idea. I wanted to create a project on the impact of different wind speeds on stationary objects," she explained. "So I created this."

When she put it together, it was a model of trees, small mountains and pools of water. "I thought if we could figure out the perfect speed to move each one, we might be able to figure out how to protect each one from harm if there's bad weather."

"Great idea!" Mr. Woods clapped his hands loudly. "Wow Bethany, I bet the meteorologist at the local news station would love to see this project. Do you mind if I tell him about it?"

"Not at all," Bethany blushed shyly.

"That really is a great project," Max said as he studied it closely. "You might be able to make a very important discovery because of this Bethany. I'm really impressed."

"You?" Bethany asked with surprise. "Really?"

"Yes really," Max laughed. "It's a whole lot better than some super green goo!"

"Green goo would be a lot more fun," Bethany pointed out.

"The important question is what happens when you combine a certain wind speed with some super green goo," Rebekah asked from behind other of them.

"Oh no!" Bethany laughed at the idea.

"You'd sure have a gooey situation," Max joked, making all three of them laugh.

"Alright kids, we need to get started with class," Mr. Woods said as he waved them to their desks. Rebekah walked slowly to her desk. She wasn't looking forward to sharing her project with the class.

Rebekah was walking to her desk when Mr. Woods called out to her. "Where's your project Rebekah?" he asked. Rebekah sighed. She picked up her book bag.

Rebekah pulled the carnation out of her book bag that she had colored with food dye.

"Not very creative, I know," she said with a frown as she laid it on Mr. Woods' desk.

"You know Rebekah, I think your project was the most creative of all," Mr. Woods said with a smile.

"A flower?" Rebekah asked with surprise.

"No not the flower, although that is fun to do," Mr. Woods grinned. "I'm talking about your mystery solving," Mr. Woods laughed. "How did you figure it out?" he asked.

"Well," Rebekah frowned. "I smelled lemon and I felt goo, and I knew there was no such thing as green goo eating vampires," she shrugged. Mr. Woods raised his eyebrows.

"Okay," he said with a slight shake of his head. "Well, that's what I mean. You used a lot of scientific techniques to figure out just what happened to Max's project. Without your senses you wouldn't have been able to figure it out.

Good job! No one else has demonstrated how science is used to solve mysteries, so I'd say that your project was very creative after all! Wouldn't you?" he asked.

"I guess so," Rebekah beamed proudly. She always knew that science was just another kind of mystery, and she was determined to solve it. She was just going to make sure she wasn't around when Bethany and Max did their wind and green goo experiment. That was one mystery she didn't have any desire to solve.

Rebekah - Girl Detective #16
Quiet On The Set!

Chapter 1

Rebekah flipped through the pages of the magazine on her bed. She was looking for pictures of one person in particular. Danny Dakota.

Danny Dakota was a big star, at least to Rebekah he was. He played a detective on the hit television show, "Justice for Kids" and she thought he was the best actor in the world.

Danny was just a year older than she was and she was amazed that he could be on television. Not only was he on television, but he was going to star in a movie about his television show. She couldn't wait for the movie to be out so that she could see it in the theater.

When her phone began ringing, Rebekah didn't want to answer it. She wanted to read an article about Danny's movie. She finally answered it on the fifth ring.

"Hello?" she said.

"Hi Rebekah, it's RJ," her cousin RJ said into the phone.

"What's going on RJ?" Rebekah asked with a smile. She always loved to hear from her older cousin. He had taught her everything she knew about being a detective. While Rebekah lived in a small town, he lived in the big city and they had a great time talking about mysteries.

"Well I heard this rumor," RJ said. Rebekah could hear the excitement in his voice.

"Rumor about what?" she asked as she sat up and pressed the phone closer to her ear.

"About Danny Dakota and his new movie," RJ replied. "I know how much you like the show, and Danny, so I thought I should tell you what I heard."

"What? What did you hear?" Rebekah asked eagerly. She was holding the phone so tightly that her fingers were going numb.

"Hensely said he saw some camera men outside of the apartment building today while I was in school. The camera men were looking for a good place to film one of the scenes for the movie. So Hensely suggested they use the lobby!" RJ said excitedly.

"The lobby of your apartment building?" Rebekah asked with a gasp. RJ's parents were the managers of the apartment building they lived in.

"Yes!" RJ laughed. "I think they're going to be shooting here this weekend. Do you think your parents would let you come visit?"

"I'll ask right now!" Rebekah squealed and hung up the phone. She ran out into the living room where her parents were watching a television show. "Can I go to RJ's this weekend?" she asked hopefully.

"Sure if you like," her mother nodded. "As long as all of your homework is done," she added.

"It will be!" Rebekah promised. She was so excited that she called RJ back right away to let him know that she would be there. She knew that she might not get to see Danny Dakota, he might not even be in the scene, but it would still be amazing to see part of the movie being filmed.

Chapter 2

Of course no matter what Rebekah did, she couldn't leave out her best friend Mouse. She called him right away to see if he could come with her to RJ's too.

Mouse's mother agreed that they could spend the night on Saturday, but on Sunday they had to be home early because it was a school night.

Rebekah was very excited when her mother drove them both to RJ's apartment building. RJ was waiting for them with a wide grin.

"Guess what?" he said as soon as they got out of the car.

"What?" Rebekah asked after hugging her mother goodbye.

"They're really going to be here!" RJ said. "First thing in the morning!"

"Oh wow!" Rebekah clapped her hands. Mouse rolled his eyes a little. "Oh you know what we have to do?" Rebekah asked with a big smile.

"What?" both RJ and Mouse asked.

"Danny Dakota marathon!" she squealed and ran into the apartment building.

"Oh no," Mouse groaned.

"What exactly is a Danny Dakota marathon?" RJ asked with a raised eyebrow.

"It's when Rebekah pulls up all of the episodes on the computer and watches them. All of them," Mouse hung his head slightly. "We're going to need snacks."

"Yes we are," RJ laughed and shook his head. "I like the Danny Dakota show, but not that much."

"Don't worry, I brought my pet mouse Hollywood. We can teach him some tricks," Mouse said as he showed RJ the mouse in his pocket.

"Oh good, but don't let my Dad see him," RJ warned. "He's a little touchy about mice in the building."

"I won't," Mouse promised.

Chapter 3

That night while RJ and Mouse taught Hollywood to run through a maze made of books and shoes to get some cheese, Rebekah watched at least ten episodes of Danny Dakota on the computer.

Even though she already knew what happened in the episode, she was still impressed when Danny Dakota figured out the mystery.

RJ and Mouse fell asleep long before Rebekah did. When she finally turned off the computer, all she could think about was Danny Dakota and all of the mysteries he solved.

The next morning she was so excited she woke RJ and Mouse up early.

They met Hensely in the lobby. Hensely pointed out all of the equipment that the staff members were bringing in. Even though they were up early, the lobby had already been filled with props and decorations.

Rebekah admired the large cameras that were rolled into position to film the scene. The lobby of RJ's apartment building was completely transformed from a run of the mill lobby to what looked like a very dark and scary mansion. It made Rebekah excited for the upcoming movie.

"Do you see him Mouse?" she whispered to her friend who was trying to keep his pet mouse in his pocket.

"Not yet," he replied with a smile. Mouse knew how much Rebekah liked Danny Dakota. Mouse didn't really enjoy the show, he liked comedies better, but he would always watch it with Rebekah if she wanted to. He thought Danny was a good actor too, but he wondered what it would be like to be a kid and have to act like someone else all day.

"Look!" Rebekah pointed with excitement. "It's Dylan Banner, he plays Danny Dakota's uncle and arch nemesis in the movie," she sighed as she watched Dylan Banner stride across the lobby. She wasn't as big of a fan of him, but if he was there, maybe Danny Dakota would be too.

"Here guys," RJ said as he brought them over two bottles of water. "We can't get upstairs for a while, so the staff is handing out water. Did you see him yet?" he asked Rebekah with a grin.

"No, maybe he won't be here," Rebekah shrugged a little. "But this is still amazing!"

"It is pretty cool," RJ admitted. He pointed to a man in a big brown hat with a red scarf tied around his neck. "That's the director," he said. "He says when they will start filming."

"Oh boy!" Rebekah took a sip of her water. "I can't wait to see this in the movies and know that I was here when they filmed it."

"Well it is exciting, but sometimes scenes don't make it into the movie," RJ warned. "It would be so cool if this did though!"

Chapter 4

"Quiet on the set!" a very tall and very thin man shrieked from the opposite corner of the lobby. Rebekah, Mouse and RJ did their best to be very quiet.

"Action!" shouted the director. Dylan Banner began pacing back and forth. It was amazing to Rebekah how he went from being just a guy walking around, to looking very evil, as if he was about to do something terrible.

"He'll never stop me," Dylan Banner chuckled darkly as he paused in the middle of the lobby. "Once and for all, I've defeated Danny Dakota."

"Think again, uncle!" a voice cried out from the other side of the lobby. When Rebekah looked up she saw that a ladder and platform had been brought into the room. Standing on top of it with a rope in his hand, was none other than Danny Dakota. Rebekah's mouth dropped open. Mouse's hand clamped over her mouth before she could let out a squeal.

"Shh," RJ reminded her in a whisper. Rebekah nodded quickly and took a breath. Danny jumped off of the platform and swung right through the lobby. He landed right on top of Dylan Banner's shoulders.

"You'll never win," he growled and covered his uncle's eyes.

"Ah!" Dylan cried out and tugged at Danny's hands. He wandered around as if he couldn't keep his balance. Rebekah was worried that Danny might get hurt. Then she saw all of the cushions that had been laid out on the floor to protect him just in case they fell.

"Look at that," Mouse whispered as he saw one of the cushions inflate. He was leaning down to get a closer look when Hollywood slipped right out of his pocket.

"Oh no," Rebekah gasped when she saw the mouse escape.

"Shh!" a member of the movie staff hissed at her.

"Peek-a-boo uncle!" Danny cried out and lifted his hands off of his uncle's eyes. Rebekah had no idea what was supposed to happen in the movie, but she was sure that what did happen had nothing to do with the movie.

Chapter 5

"Mouse!" Dylan Banner shrieked. "There's a mouse!" he began running around in a circle with Danny still on his shoulders.

"Cut!" the director called out. Rebekah slapped her forehead and closed her eyes for a moment. Mouse was trying to sneak on to the set to get Hollywood before someone with a broom could. RJ grimaced.

"Oh dad's not going to like this," he muttered under his breath.

Dylan lost his balance with Danny still on his shoulders and went tumbling down on to one of the cushions. People were running in all directions, some from the mouse and some to the mouse.

There was chaos in the lobby and some of the props even fell over. Mouse finally retrieved Hollywood and hid behind Rebekah and RJ hoping that no one would figure out that it was his mouse that caused all the commotion.

"Keep him in your pocket!" RJ said through gritted teeth. "If Dad hears about this, he's going to be upset. He's not going to want everyone to think that we have a mouse problem in our building!"

"Even if you do," Rebekah said with a roll of her eyes at mouse.

"Sorry," Mouse squeaked out. Once everyone calmed down, the staff tried to fix up the lobby so that it looked like a spooky mansion again. Then someone called out.

"Where's Danny?"

Everyone got very quiet as they looked around the room.

"Danny? Danny Dakota?" the director shouted. Some of the staff began scouring the lobby.

"Where is he?" Dylan demanded. "We have a schedule to keep!"

After a few minutes of looking, Dylan sighed. "Well he's done it again, hasn't he?" he asked with a frown. "He did this last week too. We were signing autographs and he just disappeared so he could go to an ice cream shop!"

"Don't worry," one of the staff members said. "We'll find him."

"This is ridiculous," Dylan said with a huff.

"That's what happens when you work with kids," the director shrugged. "Take five everyone."

Rebekah, RJ, and Mouse grouped together. "Where do you think he went?" Rebekah asked.

"Well Dylan Banner said he slipped away to an ice cream shop before. We should go look for him," RJ suggested.

"Good idea!" Rebekah and Mouse agreed. They left the lobby of the apartment building and began walking up and down the block. There were a few little shops, like the pizza shop, the corner store and a small deli that had ice cream too. Rebekah, RJ and Mouse spent the whole day searching.

"Oh no, Mom's going to be here soon," Rebekah frowned as she glanced at her watch.

"Don't worry, I'm sure they'll find him," RJ said.

"I hope Hollywood didn't scare him off," Mouse murmured as he patted the top of Hollywood's head.

Chapter 6

When Rebekah's mother pulled up in front of the apartment building the kids were just walking back.

"How exciting," Rebekah's mother said when she saw all the cameras and trucks. "Did you get to meet Danny Dakota?" she asked.

"No," Rebekah said with a frown. "He disappeared before I could."

"Well go grab your things and say goodbye to RJ," her mother said. "Mouse's mother is waiting for him. It's a school night and you three need to get to bed."

Rebekah's mother left the van for a moment to say hello to RJ's parents. She didn't think she needed to lock it because she was still close by. Once Rebekah and Mouse had all of their things and said goodbye to RJ they hurried back to the van. They clamored in to the middle seat, still talking about the day.

"Mom you should have seen it," Rebekah said with a sigh. "Danny Dakota swung across the lobby! He does his own stunts! How cool is that?"

"I wouldn't exactly call it a stunt," Mouse pointed out with a frown.

"Well what you pulled sure was a stunt," Rebekah whispered to him.

Mouse frowned and tucked Hollywood back into his pocket. "I just hope it wasn't the reason Danny took off."

"Is it true that Danny Dakota is missing?" Rebekah's mother asked.

"It is," Mouse nodded. "But he's disappeared before."

"I'm sure he'll be fine," Rebekah's mother said. "Poor little guy probably just needed a break."

Chapter 7

That night after they dropped Mouse off at his house, Rebekah hurried into the house. She wanted to get on the computer to check and see if Danny had been found yet.

She was in such a hurry that she left her bag in the van. When she went to unpack it, she realized it was still in the van.

"Mom, I'm just going to grab my bag," she called out as she stepped out the front door. When she walked up to the van she realized she didn't have the keys. She tried the door just in case and was surprised to find it open.

She always locked the doors and her mother always double checked. Not only was it unlocked, but it was a little bit open, as if someone didn't know that it had to be slammed to be closed.

"Strange," Rebekah muttered. But she had been so excited about Danny Dakota that she figured she must have just forgotten to lock it and close it properly. She grabbed her bag, locked the door and slammed it shut.

Then she ran back into the house. She couldn't wait to get to school the next day and tell her friend Amanda about seeing Danny Dakota in person!

Chapter 8

Rebekah waited by her locker the next day. She knew that Amanda would want to hear all about Danny Dakota. Rebekah only wished she had more to tell. She had only seen him for a few minutes.

On the news this morning they said he was still missing, but no one was too concerned because he had a reputation for running off. That made Rebekah a little sad. She thought it would hurt her feelings if she went missing and no one was worried.

"Did you see him, did you see him?" Amanda asked as she hurried up to Rebekah's locker.

"I did," Rebekah said proudly. "I mean I didn't get to meet him or anything, but I was in the same lobby as him!" she giggled.

"How amazing," Amanda sighed dreamily. "I have such a crush on him!" she gushed.

"A crush?" Rebekah scrunched up her nose. "Ew!"

"Oh stop, you like him as much as I do!" Amanda rolled her eyes.

"No, ma'am," Rebekah shook her head firmly. "I respect his detective work. That's it!"

"You do know he's just an actor right Rebekah?" Amanda laughed.

"Well, I bet he likes to solve real mysteries too," Rebekah said with confidence. She knew a thing or two about solving mysteries and she was sure that Danny did too. As they walked to class Rebekah told Amanda about Hollywood escaping and Danny's disappearance.

"I hope he's okay," Amanda frowned.

"Me too," Rebekah nodded and opened the door to their classroom. When they walked in most of the other kids were already sitting at their desks.

One boy was sitting all the way in the back row with the hood of his sweatshirt pulled down over his head. Rebekah only noticed him because he was tapping his fingernails nervously on the desk. She wasn't sure who he was, which was strange, because she knew all of the kids in her class.

During the class she waited for the teacher to introduce the new student, but she never did. She didn't even seem to notice him in the back of the class. Rebekah found this very suspicious.

Chapter 9

When class was over, Rebekah waited until all of the other kids left the room. The boy was still sitting at his desk, as if he was waiting for her to leave. Rebekah fiddled with her book bag.

Finally the boy got up and walked out of the class. Rebekah waited a few moments and then followed after him.

As she suspected he walked to her next class. Just as before he took the desk all the way in the back. Once again her teacher didn't seem to notice him and didn't introduce him.

Rebekah raised her hand.

"Yes Rebekah?" Mr. Woods her science teacher asked.

"Mr. Woods aren't you going to-" she glanced over at the boy. He put his finger to his lips. Rebekah wasn't sure what to do. She wanted to know who he was, but she didn't really want to get him in trouble. "Give us our homework assignment?" Rebekah asked.

"Oh yes, thank you for reminding me," Mr. Woods laughed. "I almost forgot, can't have that!" All of the other kids in the class glared at Rebekah for making sure they had homework.

Rebekah was staring at the boy in the back of the class. When the bell rang Rebekah hung back, but this time the boy was one of the first ones to leave the classroom. Rebekah followed after him, but by the time she reached the hall he was gone.

"How strange," she whispered to herself. She was determined to find out who the boy was. She noticed Mouse at his locker.

"Mouse, there's this new boy in my classes and I can't figure out who he is," Rebekah said with a frown as she walked up beside him.

"Well have you asked him his name?" Mouse asked as he stacked up his books.

"Uh, no," Rebekah laughed a little. She hadn't even thought of just introducing herself.

"Well that's usually a good way to meet someone," Mouse winked at her. "Have to hurry," he said as he waved over his shoulder.

Chapter 10

Rebekah's next class was gym. She changed into her gym clothes and then joined her friend Jaden in some basketball before class started. As she was shooting the ball into the hoop she noticed someone staring at her from the bleachers.

When she looked up she saw the boy with the hood pulled up over his head. She was so distracted that when Jaden passed her the ball, it bounced right off the side of her head.

"Ouch!" she gasped and lost her balance. She fell hard on the gym floor.

"I'm so sorry!" she heard Jaden call. But when she opened her eyes, she was looking right up at Danny Dakota.

"Are you okay?" he asked her with a frown.

"I'm okay," she replied. She glanced over at Jaden to see if he saw Danny Dakota too, but when she looked back, Danny was gone. She blinked and sat up, rubbing her head.

"Rebekah I didn't mean it honest," Jaden said as he crouched down next to her.

"Did you see him?" Rebekah asked as she stared around the gym.

"See who?" Jaden wondered.

"Danny Dakota," Rebekah replied.

"The actor?" Jaden shook his head. "Maybe you need to see the nurse Rebekah."

"Maybe I do," she sighed.

Chapter 11

For the rest of the school day Rebekah searched for Danny Dakota. She didn't see the boy in the hooded sweatshirt at all. She even asked Mouse to look for him too.

"I'm sure it was Danny Dakota Mouse," she told him at lunch.

"And you had just been hit in the head with a basketball," Mouse reminded her with a frown.

"I know, I know," Rebekah sighed. "But I looked right at him. He asked me if I was okay!"

"Why would Danny Dakota ever come here?" Mouse asked with a shake of his head.

"I don't know, but think about it," Rebekah insisted. "He disappeared after Hollywood escaped. Mom left the van alone while she talked to RJ's parents. Then that night after I got home I went back out to get my bag and the door to the van was open!"

"That is odd," Mouse said. "But still, if you were a Hollywood star and you wanted to run away, would it be to school?" he asked with a grin.

"Probably not," Rebekah admitted. "It does seem strange. But I know what I saw," she said firmly.

"Well I'll help you look," Mouse said. "But don't get your hopes too high Rebekah, big stars like Danny Dakota don't disappear so they can go to school."

Even though Mouse and Rebekah looked everywhere for Danny, they couldn't find him. Rebekah didn't see the boy in the hooded shirt in any more of her classes.

She felt a little sad on the way home, but the more she thought about it, the more sure she was that she had seen Danny. He had looked right at her after all!

She knew she needed the help of another detective, so when she got home she called her cousin RJ.

"RJ," Rebekah said when he answered the phone. "Danny Dakota is here! He's in our town."

"What?" RJ asked with surprise. "Are you sure about that?"

"Yes I'm sure, I saw him at school today," Rebekah said quickly.

"At school? Why would Danny Dakota be at school?" he asked.

"I don't know, but that's where I saw him," Rebekah replied with certainty.

"Do you know where he is now?" RJ asked curiously. "Everyone is still looking for him. If you know where he is, you should probably tell someone."

"I don't know," Rebekah frowned. "I lost him after I got hit with a basketball."

"You were hit with a basketball?" RJ asked with surprise. Rebekah, did you really see him or did you just think you saw him?" RJ asked. "After all those episodes you watched he's probably stuck in your brain."

"I really saw him," Rebekah insisted. "You have to believe me RJ, I'm not making this up."

"I believe you Rebekah," RJ knew his younger cousin was one of the best detectives around. "Well what do you think he's doing there?" RJ asked with confusion. "Maybe he has amnesia and doesn't remember who he is?"

"Maybe," Rebekah sighed. "I just hope wherever he is, he has a safe place to stay."

Chapter 12

As the day got later, Rebekah got more worried about Danny. She knew he couldn't stay in the school all night because there were janitors and security guards.

She didn't think he'd have anywhere to be safe, or maybe even any food to eat. She sat down on her bed and tried to think about what she would do if she was hiding out and had no one to help her.

She would try to find a safe place where no one would look for her. Since kids are less likely to be suspicious, she would probably hide out where kids were instead of adults. The only places she could think that kids would be, were school and the playground.

Then she would probably want to be somewhere close to food. She remembered that there was a little store not far from the playground that sold all kinds of snacks and ice cream. If she was hiding out, she would definitely hide near the playground. But she would also need a place to sleep.

"Hm," she said thoughtfully. "I wouldn't be able to sleep on the swings and the slide would be pretty uncomfortable. Plus, what if it rained?" she tapped her chin for a moment. Then suddenly she knew exactly where Danny was. She grabbed her jacket.

"Mom, I'll be back before dark!" she called to her mother as she ran out the door. She ran all the way to Mouse's house and pounded on his door.

"Rebekah?" Mouse asked with surprise. "Why are you knocking so loudly?"

"I think I know where he is," Rebekah said with a wide smile. "Come on Mouse, let's go find him!"

"Where is he?" Mouse asked as he followed after Rebekah. "Are you sure you know where he is?"

"I'm sure," Rebekah said with confidence. "Follow me!"

She led Mouse to the park, which was mostly empty as it was getting dark. She walked across the open field to the trees.

"Rebekah, where are you going?" Mouse asked as he followed after her. "I don't think a television star is going to be hiding out in the trees."

"Maybe not in the trees," Rebekah said in a whisper as she stopped in front of the tree house where Mouse held meetings of his secret club. "Maybe in a tree house," she pointed up to the tree house where a small light was shining. Mouse's eyes widened.

"Do you really think he's up there?" he asked.

"Only one way to find out," Rebekah replied and began climbing up the rope ladder to the tree house. When she reached the top and peeked over the edge, she spotted what was making the light. There was a flashlight on the table in the middle of the tree house.

Chapter 13

"Hello?" Rebekah called out as she climbed the rest of the way up into the tree house. "Is anyone up here?"

"Go away!" a muffled voice shouted back from the corner of the tree house.

Mouse climbed up right behind Rebekah.

"We're not going anywhere," Mouse said firmly. "You're trespassing."

"Go away!" the voice shouted again. Mouse ducked his head and tried to see through the shadows into the corner. When he leaned over, the mouse in his pocket slipped out. It ran across the floor of the tree house.

"Hollywood!" Mouse said with a frown.

"Ah! What's that?" the voice cried out as the mouse ran toward the corner. "Is that a mouse? A real mouse?" the voice demanded.

"It's okay, he won't hurt you," Rebekah promised him as she scooped up the small white mouse. "He's a nice mouse," she added as she handed Mouse's pet back to him. "Now, what are you doing up here all alone?" she asked the boy huddled in the corner.

"That's just it, I want to be alone," the boy replied. "Please go away."

"I'm sorry, I can't do that Danny," Rebekah said with a shake of her head.

"Why not?" Danny asked in a growl.

"Because it's not safe for you to sleep in this tree house," Rebekah insisted. "Even if you are Danny Dakota."

"You know who I am?" Danny gasped with surprise. "Did you tell anyone? Any reporters?"

"No reporters," Rebekah shook her head. "Only my cousin and my friend Mouse here know who you are."

"Oh good," Danny sighed. "But I guess you're going to tell, huh?"

"I won't tell anyone," Rebekah promised. "If you tell me why you're hiding out like this."

"The truth is, I needed a break," Danny said. "I just wanted to be a normal kid for a few days."

"Well then you're in the wrong tree house," Mouse laughed.

"I'm sorry, I've never had the chance to go to a real school," Danny explained with a shake of his head. "I've been working in television for so long that sometimes I forget what it's like to just be a kid," he frowned as he looked at them.

"Well we can change that," Rebekah said with a smile. "But you can't sleep in a tree house."

"He can sleep at my house," Mouse offered. "Then we can all go to school together tomorrow."

"I think that's a great idea," Rebekah agreed. "What do you think Danny?"

Danny smiled and nodded. "Sounds good to me. I can't wait to go to school again!"

Chapter 14

The next day at school Rebekah and Mouse showed Danny all the fun things about being in school and some of the not so fun things. Danny had a great time meeting their friends, even Amanda, who nearly fainted when she saw him.

They all promised to keep his secret. But by the end of the day, Danny was worn out.

"I don't know how you do this every day," he laughed as he looked at the stack of homework he'd been given. "School might be a lot of fun, but it's a lot of work too."

"Well Danny if you want to stay, we can help you stay," Rebekah offered with a smile.

"It's been great," Danny admitted. "But my fans are looking forward to that new movie."

"Yes we are!" Rebekah said happily.

"So I better get back to work," he sighed. He pulled out his cell phone to call for his agent to come pick him up. "Thanks guys for showing me what it's like to be a normal kid."

"Normal?" Mouse raised an eyebrow.

Danny laughed. "This is one adventure I won't ever forget."

"Just remember," Rebekah said as she walked him out of the school. "If you decide to base a character in your movie or television show on me, it's Rebekah with a 'k' and you can leave out the whole basketball hitting me in the head part."

"You got it, Rebekah," he smiled and shook her hand. "I'll make sure you all have passes to the premier of the movie."

"Thanks Danny!" Rebekah waved to him as he climbed into his agent's car. She was happy to have met him and even happier that she knew just what it was like to be a normal kid. Well, a normal kid that was also a detective, of course.

Next Steps

I really hope that you've enjoyed this collection of stories and I'd love to hear from you at the Facebook page below - please do stop by and let us know how you are enjoying the books!

Rebekah - Girl Detective:
http://www.facebook.com/RebekahGirlDetective

I very much appreciate your reviews and comments so thank you in advance for taking a moment to leave one for "Rebekah - Girl Detective: Books 13-16."

Sincerely,
PJ Ryan

Visit the author website for a complete list of all titles available.

PJRyanBooks.com

Now Available in Audio

Several of the PJ Ryan titles are now available as audiobooks!

Visit the author website for a complete list at:
PJRyanBooks.com

You can also listen to free audio samples there.

Titles by PJ Ryan Can be Found Here
PJRyanBooks.com
*Visit the author page to save big on special bundled sets!

****

"Rebekah - Girl Detective"
#1 The Mysterious Garden
#2 Alien Invasion
#3 Magellan Goes Missing
#4 Ghost Hunting
#5 Grown-Ups Out To Get Us?!
#6: The Missing Gems
#7: Swimming With Sharks?!
#8: Magic Gone Wrong!
#9: Mystery At Summer Camp
#10: Zombie Burgers
#11: Mouse's Secret
#12: The Missing Ice Cream
#13: The Ghost Snowman
#14: Monkey Business
#15: Science Magic
#16: Quiet On The Set!

"RJ - Boy Detective"
#1: The Mysterious Crate
#2: Vampire Hunting
#3: Alien Goo!
#4: Mystery Poo
#5: Mr. Pip Is Missing!
#6: Where Is Hensely?
#7: Night Noises
#8: The Cheese Thief

"Mouse's Secret Club"
#1: Let It Snow (Inside the Gym!)
#2: Haunted Playground
#3: Spotted!
#4: Magnificent Marvin
#5: Picnic Prank
#6: Fun House
#7: It's A Bird!
#8: Mouse Ninja!

"Rebekah, Mouse & RJ: Special Editions"
Prank Gone Wrong
Halloween Haunted House
Thanksgiving Turkey Trouble
Christmas Party Mystery
Birthday Surprise
Happy New Year!
Playing Cupid: A Valentine's Day Surprise
Leprechaun Hunting: A St. Patrick's Day Mystery
The Easter Egg Hunt

This is a work of fiction. The characters, incidents and locations portrayed in this book and the names herein are fictitious. Any similarity to or identification with the locations, names, characters or history of any person, product or entity is entirely coincidental and unintentional.

From a Declaration of Principles jointly adopted by a Committee of the American Bar Association and a Committee of Publishers and Associations.

All rights reserved. No part of this publication may be reproduced or transmitted in any form or by any means, electronic or mechanical, including photocopy, recording, or any information storage or retrieval system, without permission in writing from the publisher.

No responsibility or liability is assumed by the Publisher for any injury, damage or financial loss sustained to persons or property from the use of this information, personal or otherwise, either directly or indirectly. While every effort has been made to ensure reliability and accuracy of the information within, all liability, negligence or otherwise, from any use, misuse or abuse of the operation of any methods, strategies, instructions or ideas contained in the material herein, is the sole responsibility of the reader.

Any copyrights not held by publisher are owned by their respective authors.

All information is generalized, presented for informational purposes only and presented "as is" without warranty or guarantee of any kind.

All trademarks and brands referred to in this book are for illustrative purposes only, are the property of their respective owners and not affiliated with this publication in any way. Any trademarks are being used without permission, and the publication of the trademark is not authorized by, associated with or sponsored by the trademark owner.

Made in the USA
Middletown, DE
09 November 2020

23617673R00073